THE DOMINIE WORLD OF
OCEAN LIFE
ANTARCTICA

Friends in the Sea

WRITTEN & PHOTOGRAPHED
BY KIM WESTERSKOV, Ph.D.

DOMINIE PRESS
Pearson Learning Group

1

Sea Lions

Sea lions love playing with each other, with people, dogs, or anything, it seems. With whales, even! They sometimes climb up onto the wide backs of right whales. When the huge whale rises out of the sea, the sea lions slide back into the water—they then climb onboard the whale to do it all over again.

Sea lions are wonderful, **agile**, and fast swimmers. Watching a group of them is like watching a graceful underwater ballet. I could watch them for hours, and sometimes I do.

◂ *"Come on in and join us," these three sea lions seem to be saying.*

NOTES

Sea lions are probably my favorite friends in the sea. They like swimming with me as much as I like being with them. Sometimes when I am swimming near a beach where they are resting, they will come out and join me, just for the fun of it—as far as I can tell.

There are five **species** of sea lions in the world. The best known is the California sea lion, the trained seal you might see in zoos, marine parks, and circuses. The others are the Steller's, South American, Australian, and New Zealand sea lions. The champion diver among all the fur seals and sea lions is the New Zealand sea lion, one I have dived with many times. Normal dives are 400 feet deep, but this champion can reach depths of 2,000 feet. It is also the world's rarest sea lion. About 10,000 to 15,000 of these amazing creatures live on small islands south of New Zealand.

NOTES

"Nibbling my flipper" is one of the sea lion's favorite games. So, too, is "nibbling my elbow," "nibbling my fingers," and any other part of me that they can get their mouth around. These nibbles are gentle and not meant to hurt—they are all just a form of play.

▲ *Rest takes up a big part of every day for sea lion pups. Growing is such tiring work!*

2

Sea Lion Pups

Baby seals and sea lions are called **pups**. I love sea lion pups. In many ways they are like kittens or puppies: they have big round eyes, they are very cute, playful, and inquisitive, and they have a lot of fun. They sleep, feed on mother's milk, play, explore, play-fight… and then sleep again.

Sea lions breed in **colonies** on sandy beaches or rocky shores. The mother is at least four years old before she has her first pup,

A big pup in a rock pool wades near the shore, always ready to explore and play.

and only one is born at a time. Mother and pup stay close to each other for the first week or two. About ten to fifteen days after giving birth, the mother returns to the sea to feed herself. She will return every few days to nurse the pup, feeding it with her rich milk. As the pup gets older, the mother's feeding trips become longer. The pup **suckles** for at least six to twelve months, and in one species for up to three years.

While the mothers are feeding themselves at sea, the pups stay on the beach, sleeping, playing, and exploring. The pups start swimming when they are only a few weeks old. At first they splash around in rock pools or streams, or at the sea's edge. Soon, they are following their mothers out to sea, where they learn to feed. The sea lion's **diet** includes a variety of seafood: fish, octopus, squid, crabs, krill, and sometimes penguins.

NOTES

I sat down on the rocks near a group of large pups playing in shallow pools. A few of them were curious and came over to see me. This one rubbed itself against my boots, and nibbled them with its sharp teeth.

3

Sea Lion Bulls

Sea lion pups are fun to be with, but the **bulls** are not. They are big, fast, and scary. On a flat, sandy beach they sometimes charge straight at me, mouths open and roaring loudly. They can run surprisingly fast, so I move away quickly. Luckily, they don't chase me for long. As soon as they see me running, they seem to think, "I've won!" and stop following me.

NOTES

Once I was diving with a group of about twenty sea lions near their colony. Most were females and youngsters. One young bull had an even better idea. He swam down from above, grabbed my head in his jaws, and held me there, without moving.

His hold was gentle enough not to hurt me, but firm enough so that I could not move. Some minutes went by. The sea lion was still holding on to my head. I was wondering, "So what happens next?" Eventually, another diver jumped in from our boat not far away. The bull let go of my head and swam over to check out this new playmate. When I looked closely at my wetsuit hood, I could see four holes right through it. I'm very pleased that he was only playing!

◂ *A bull sea lion charges at full speed and roars—a frightening sight. Time to get out of the way quickly! Better still not to have gotten so close to begin with.*

A bull sea lion sits beside a pup on the beach. Sea lions have blunt snouts, or noses, while fur seals have pointed snouts. ▾

Maybe the young bulls are practicing for the time when they will be in a breeding colony, where only one bull will become the "beach master" of that part of the beach and all the females there. They do this by fighting and chasing all the other bulls away. Being a beach master is hard work.

Beach masters do not eat during the breeding season, but stay guarding "their" beach and "their" females, day after day. No wonder they seem bad-tempered!

NOTES

Bull sea lions are much more aggressive than females and youngsters. They swim straight toward me at high speed, with their mouths open, showing me their sharp teeth. Just before they reach me, they veer to one side. They pass so close that I could reach out and touch them, if I wanted to.

4

Fur Seals

CAUTION!

If you ever meet fur seals or sea lions on the shore, just watch them quietly from a safe distance. Definitely don't try to touch or feed them, or get between the seal and the sea. Fur seals and sea lions can be aggressive. They can move fast, their teeth are sharp, and their bite is powerful. Even the pups!

Fur seal pups are almost as likeable as sea lion pups, but they aren't as friendly toward humans. If I don't get too close and I move slowly, they get used to me and start playing their seal pup games: play-fighting, chasing each other, and racing around their rock pools at high speed.

Two fur seal pups are wet after playing in a large, shallow rock pool. Fur seals have sharper, more pointed snouts than sea lions. ▸

In many ways, fur seals and sea lions are similar, but there are some differences. Fur seals have longer, more pointed **snouts** than the rounded snouts of sea lions. They are usually smaller, too.

There are nine species of fur seals. Most live in cold seas in the **southern hemisphere**. Northern fur seals make long migrations each year, between Alaska, where they breed, and California. In all species, the bulls are larger than the **cows**—up to five times heavier.

A fur seal's year is very similar to a sea lion's. In spring and summer, fur seals come ashore in groups on rocky coastlines to **mate** and have their young. Cows give birth to one baby a year, feeding it with their warm milk. Mothers and pups know each other's voices and smells, and they can easily find each other after the mother gets back from her feeding trips.

While waiting for Mom to return from the sea, fur seal pups sometimes gather in groups called crèches. ▸

5

Fur Seals Underwater

Fur seals and sea lions use their long front flippers to **propel** their **streamlined** bodies powerfully through the water. Their hind flippers are used for steering.

▲ *A fur seal heads straight toward the camera at high speed.*

Fur seals are excellent divers, some species easily reaching depths of 600 feet, and sometimes 1,000 feet. Their favorite foods are squid, octopus, fish, and the occasional penguin. Many of their **prey** come nearer to the surface at night, so fur seals often dive throughout the night. Their sharp teeth are good for catching prey, but not for chewing. They normally swallow their prey whole, in one big gulp.

This fur seal is hanging upside down at the surface of a kelp bed. ▸

Seal pups become good swimmers at an early age. As soon as the pup can keep up with its mother, she heads out to sea, taking her pup with her to teach it how to swim, feed, and avoid **predators**. Young fur seals are sometimes found over 600 miles away from where they were born.

NOTES

Swimming with fur seals is much like swimming with sea lions, except that sea lions are definitely more fun. I don't know why, but fur seals are just not as playful. They swim just as beautifully, though, using their flippers to turn, twist, change direction, and zoom straight toward me at high speed.

6

Elephant Seals and Leopard Seals

Elephant seals are the largest of all seals. Adult males normally grow to sixteen feet, and occasionally twenty feet! Their maximum weight is about four tons. Adult females are seven to ten feet long and weigh up to nearly a ton.

On land, elephant seals look like huge, sleepy, and somewhat ugly slugs. But that first impression is quite unfair. The pups are both cute and playful, and the adults are fast and graceful in the sea. Elephant seals travel widely and spend up to eight months at sea at one time.

At sea, elephant seals dive almost nonstop, day and night. A normal dive for an elephant

NOTES

I'm not sure about calling these seals "friends," but let's meet them, anyway. They are fascinating animals. I was a little nervous when I met a large elephant seal underwater, but only because of its size. It ignored me totally as I admired it for a while, and then it left.

◂ *"This is my beach!" A bull elephant seal pushes its way ashore between two inflatable boats.*

▾ *A group of large bull elephant seals rests on the beach.*

▲ *A leopard seal shows its sharp teeth.*

seal lasts for about half an hour and can reach depths of 2,000 feet. After a few minutes on the surface between dives, the seal goes back down again, searching for more large fish and squid. Elephant seals can reach depths of 6,500 feet and stay down for two hours. During a deep dive, their heart rate drops to as little as one single beat per minute.

I have not yet met a leopard seal underwater, and it's the one seal I'm not in a hurry to meet. Leopard seals are the only seals that **prey** on other seals, and they have been known to attack humans. They are fast, fierce hunters, eating mostly seals—usually young crab eater seals—penguins, and krill.

7

Weddell Seals

All seal pups are so likeable that I find it hard not to fall in love with all of them. The favorites of many people are the beautiful white pups of harp seals, which live in the icy seas of the North Atlantic Ocean. My favorite is the Weddell seal, which lives in Antarctica. Weddell seals are good looking seals, in a chubby kind of way, and they don't mind people getting close to them. I've been lucky enough to dive with them under the Antarctic sea ice.

▲ *A Weddell seal pup scratches itself while lying next to its mother on the sea ice.*

The pups are born on the sea ice in spring. They quickly snuggle next to their mother and start feeding. Weighing about sixty pounds when born, the pups grow quickly—four to five pounds per day, feeding only on their mother's white, creamy milk.

The mother stops feeding the pups six or seven weeks after they are born. By that time, the large pups are able to look after themselves. They can already stay underwater for five minutes at a time and dive to depths of 300 feet—much deeper than I have ever dived!

The Weddell seal is one of the world's best divers. Only the much bigger elephant seal and some whales are known to dive deeper and for longer periods of time. Their prey lives mostly on the **seafloor**, so feeding dives are often deep, sometimes to depths of 2,500 feet. The longest known dive was one hour and twenty-two minutes.

Very few forms of life can **survive** in Antarctica all year—some small plants, a few tiny insects, the emperor penguin, and the Weddell seal. The Weddell seal relies on a very thick layer of fat and escaping into the sea whenever it gets too cold. Seawater at freezing point is still much warmer than minus sixty degrees Fahrenheit in a storm.

▲ *Mother and pup stay close for the first few months.*

A Weddell seal surfaces in its breathing hole through thick sea ice. These holes are kept open all year. ▶

8

Dolphins

Dolphins are definitely our friends, and have been for a long time. There are many true stories about dolphins helping people in trouble: keeping them afloat, protecting them from sharks, and helping them back to their boat or to shore. There is not a single reported case of dolphins harming people.

▲ *A bottlenose dolphin swims with a diver.*

Stories of special friendships between dolphins and humans have been around for at least 2,000 years. Ancient Greeks and Romans thought that harming a dolphin was as wrong as harming a person.

Today, many people swim with dolphins and enjoy watching them leaping high out of the water, surfing in on waves, or speeding alongside boats. Dolphins seem to

▾ *"Maui," the bottlenose dolphin, plays seaweed games with a swimmer. There are many stories from around the world about dolphins that have left their own kind to seek the company of humans. Most of these lone dolphins are bottlenose dolphins.*

know how to enjoy life and have fun, often better than we do. Play is common among the young of most mammals, while most adults don't play much. But among dolphins, the adults play, too.

Dolphins invent games and play with anything they can find: live fish, dead fish, seaweed, driftwood… anything. They play among themselves, with whales, or with people. There's something magical about being with dolphins. Swimming with dolphins, or even just watching them, has changed the lives of many people forever.

There are now many people who are trying hard to save dolphins and whales, and to protect the seas they live in. Dolphins have been true "friends in the sea" for thousands of years. Now it's our turn to help them, to really be *their* friends.

NOTES

So what have humans done for dolphins? Over the past forty years, tuna fishing nets have killed six to twelve million dolphins. Many more have died in other kinds of fishing nets. Dolphins are caught for food in some countries, and caught for marine parks, where half of them die within two years. We pollute the seas with our garbage and chemicals, which weaken and kill them. We also overfish the seas, robbing dolphins of their source of food. It's a long and sorry list.

9

Humpback Whales

I have swum with humpback whales many times. My best meetings were with baby whales, just weeks or a few months old. At this age they are curious and sometimes swim over to take a look at that "new animal" in the water—me! Their mother is always nearby, sometimes just keeping an eye on things, or getting between me and her baby to protect it.

▲ *A baby whale swims slowly toward the camera.*

Once I got too close to a baby humpback whale when it swam toward me. The mother swam in quickly and got between me and her baby. She was so close that her long fin was about to hit me as she swam past. But she lifted the fin to avoid hitting me. Some seconds later, the mother's **tail fluke** was about to hit me—I was still that close. I was amazed to see the mother lifting her tail fin, again so that it would not hit me.

Our "cuddle" finished, the baby whale raises its flipper, letting me go, and keeps on swimming.

My best encounter with a humpback whale was the time I was "cuddled" by a baby. I was swimming near our yacht off a tropical island in the South Pacific Ocean. I looked around me: nothing but warm, clear blue sea in every direction. Then a young whale appeared out of the depths. It saw me and turned, swimming almost straight toward me. Quite deliberately, it caught me with its long flipper, close to its "armpit," where the fin joined the body. We looked into each other's eyes, less than two feet apart, as it swam along. After some time it raised its flipper and let me go. It then swam back to its mother. She had been under us the whole time and was now swimming ahead. Wow! I had been "cuddled" by a baby humpback whale!

10

Orcas—Killer Whales

Orcas, or killer whales, are probably the sea's "ultimate predator." They are **ruthless**, powerful, fast, and very intelligent. They often work in packs, the way wolves do on land. Orcas hunt and kill several hundred different species of prey, including fish, squid, sharks, stingrays, turtles, seals, sea lions, penguins, and at least twenty species of dolphins and whales.

▲ *Orca*

But there is one remarkable thing about orcas. They are, indeed, fierce hunters of many kinds of sea animals, but they leave humans alone. There is no known case of an orca ever killing a human in the wild. Their record so far is perfect, but they are still wild animals. Why don't they eat humans? I don't know, nor do any experts I've asked. But I'm very glad the orcas don't find divers appetizing.

Humans have caught and killed many thousands of orcas over hundreds of years—and still these powerful predators have not "fought back." In the sea I found them to be curious, even playful.

NOTES

I thought about it for years before finally getting in the water with orcas. I have never really been afraid of any animals I've met in the sea, not even sharks swimming straight toward me. But when three orcas swam straight toward me, all of a sudden I was frightened. There was something scary about them: their size, a feeling of their power, and a feeling of being stalked by "predators." Back on the yacht a little later, I found that I was shaking, something that had never happened to me in the sea before.

I also realized that the orcas had not done anything at all to harm me—they were just curious. I swam with this pod many more times that day, and by the end of the day I felt almost comfortable in the water with them. They were clearly playing, with each other and with me.

▲ *Three orcas swim toward me. The middle one is carrying a stingray it caught on the seafloor. This pod is well- known for liking stingrays, often chasing them into harbors and shallow water to catch them.*

Two orcas both hang on to the same fish that one of them has caught. They are not moving, just hanging still in the water. Is this a kind of game? I guess so. ▶

11

Right Whales

These are BIG friends! Right whales are among the heaviest animals ever to have lived on Earth. Reaching a maximum of about 100 tons, this is about the same size as bowhead and fin whales. Only the mighty blue whale is bigger.

So, why do I call them "friends?" Because I like them, and I like swimming with them. They are gentle giants: slow, curious, and friendly. As with humpback whales, I have seen them carefully avoiding hitting

NOTES

My best meeting was on my birthday, July 26th, in calm waters near a subantarctic island. There was snow on the nearby hills. A dry suit kept me warm, both in our small boat and in the water.

My boatman took me out to clear water at the entrance of the harbor. Close to shore, I saw and heard whales. I slipped over the side and into the cold, clear water, and waited.

Then two whales appeared: a mother and her baby. The mother tried to shepherd the baby away from me, but the baby was curious. It wanted a close look at me. It swam up over mother's back and came straight toward me. It got bigger and bigger, until all I could see out of my facemask was a big eye and the side of a whale moving slowly past me. Although a baby, it was fifteen feet long and already weighed over a ton. What a birthday present!

swimmers or boats with their powerful tail flukes as they swam past.

Late one misty evening, three "teenage" right whales that were "hanging out" together came and swam around the small, inflatable boat that I was in. One of them gently nudged the boat. At one stage, all three whales poked their heads high out of the water—one on each side of the boat, and one behind.

When one whale swam under the boat, it was so close that its large tail fluke was going to hit the boat, and maybe accidentally knock us into the water. But just in time, the whale raised its fluke so it missed the boat—by inches. It knew exactly what it was doing. It was quite deliberate. Right whales are giants, but they are gentle giants.

The baby whale keeps on swimming.

THE DOMINIE WORLD OF OCEAN LIFE

ANTARCTICA

Glossary

Aggressive:	Showing a tendency to attack or do harm to others
Agile:	Able to move quickly and with skill and control
Bulls:	Adult males
Colonies:	Groups of animals of the same kind that live together and are dependent on one another
Cows:	Adult females
Diet:	The food that an animal or a person usually eats
Mate:	To join with another animal in order to produce offspring
Predators:	Animals that hunt, catch, and eat other animals
Prey (n):	Animals that are hunted and eaten by other animals
Prey (v):	To stalk, or hunt, an animal or a group of animals
Propel:	To move something forward
Pups:	Young animals
Ruthless:	Seeming to have no compassion or mercy
Seafloor:	The surface of the Earth at the bottom of the sea
Snout:	The part of an animal's head consisting of the nose and mouth
Southern Hemisphere:	The half of the Earth located south of the equator
Species:	Types of animals that have some physical characteristics in common
Streamlined:	Designed to move very quickly and gracefully
Suckle:	To drink a mother's milk; to nurse
Survive:	To stay alive and thrive
Tail Fluke:	The part of a whale or dolphin's tail used to propel the animal through the water